THE Forever Street Fairies

Elfie's Magic See-Saw

Written by

Hiawyn
Oram

Illustrated by

Mary
Rees

h

Hodder
Children's
Books

A division of Hodder Headline Limited

CUZ

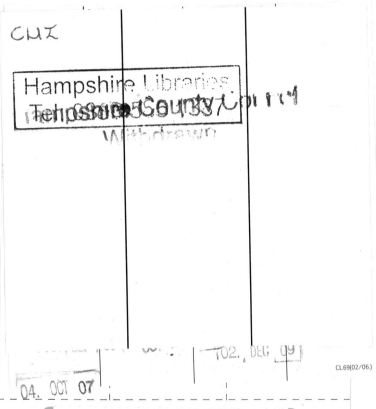

This book is due for return on or before the last date shown
above: it may, subject to the book not being reserved by
another reader, be renewed by personal application, post, or
telephone, quoting this date and details of the book.

HAMPSHIRE COUNTY COUNCIL
County Library

 100% recycled paper

Also in the series:
The Fairies Arrive
A Cake for Miss Wand
Nogo and his Muffling Magic

THE FOREVER STREET FAIRIES: ELFIE'S MAGIC SEE-SAW

by Hiawyn Oram and Mary Rees

British Library Cataloguing in Publication Data

A catalogue record of this book is available from

the British Library.

ISBN 0 340 84139 7

First edition published 2003

10 9 8 7 6 5 4 3 2 1

Published by Hodder Children's Books
a division of Hodder Headline Limited
338 Euston Road London NW1 3BH

Printed in Hong Kong

Contents

· · · · · · · · · ·

Chapter One

Bristle's Too Busy To Play

Elfie jumped on to
his magic toy box.
"Sprinkle, sprankle, sproy,"
he sang out.
"Today's magic toy will be...
something to *see* up and down on!"
He opened the box.
And there was a see-saw.

He set it up near
the Forever Street path.
At once two magic clouds
appeared above it.
"Now all I need is someone
to play with me!" cried Elfie,
and off he went looking.

2

He found Bristle
helping his magic brush
sweep Miss Wand's doorstep.
"Hello!" said Elfie.
"Where is everyone?"
"At Rainbow's," said Bristle.
"Then will YOU come and play
with me?" Elfie begged.

"Sorry," said Bristle. "After this I've got to sweep Rainbow's kitchen and spring clean Puffball's bottle!"

"Please," said Elfie. "Just for once."

"That step is spotless anyway," said Reggie the Rat from the bushes.

"Maybe it is," said Bristle. "But now I'm going over to Rainbow's. Coming, Elfie?"

Chapter Two

. . . .

Rainbow's Rat Worries

They found Rainbow sitting up in
bed with the others gathered round.
"If you're ill," said Elfie,
"a good play on my see-saw
is sure to make you feel better!"

Rainbow pulled the sheet
over her head.
"I'm not going anywhere.
Not with all my worries."
"WHAT worries?" said Elfie.
"Rat worries," said Speedwell.
"She thinks the rats are stealing
from Miss Wand's shop!"
"Well, ARE they?" said Bristle.

"That's what we have to
find out," said Fingers.
"But who'd dare stand up
to the rats?" said Elfie.
"I would!" said Fingers.
"With a little help from the twins
and Cyclone!

Come along, Pea and Pod.
It's time that White Beast
did something useful!"

Chapter Three

Elfie Takes What He Shouldn't

As Fingers went off with the twins Elfie tried to get one of the others to play with him.

"It'll be such fun," he begged. We'll see-eee up into the magic clouds and see what we'll see. Please!"

But they all had other things to do.

So Elfie hung round Bristle
while he cleaned Rainbow's kitchen.
"But you NEED to play," he argued.
You're always too busy."
"Of course I am," said Bristle.
"That's my magic."

But still Elfie didn't give up.
He followed Bristle
to Puffball's bottle house...

and hung around while Bristle
sent Puffball for a walk
and started cleaning.

"I'll even help you,"
he called into the bottle,
"if you'll play with me afterwards."
At this Bristle re-appeared,
to grab a mop and pail
and disappeared again, mumbling,
"Sorry! Just too busy!"

Elfie was about to give up.
Then he saw that Bristle
had dropped his magic
brush and pan in the grass.
"Ah ha!" said Elfie. "Without these,
he CAN'T be too busy!"
And, wrapping them
in his cloak, he ran off!

Chapter Four

. . . .

Waking Cyclone

Meanwhile, Fingers and the
Peaspods had found Cyclone
sunning himself by the fishpond.
Fingers explained what she wanted
the twins to do.

"Tickle his nose
and wake him.
Then flutter after me
making sure he follows!"
"To where?" said the twins.

"You'll see!" said Fingers.
The Peaspods twittered.
It was such a daring plan.

The White Beast's paws
were very strong.
They had to be brave
and keep out
of reach.
So holding on
to each other,
they fluttered
round his sleepy head.

At once, he woke,
growled softly,
rose up,
pawed the air,
and tried
to swat them.

14

Then setting off after Fingers,
they led him into the woods.
But as soon as Fingers was through
the gate, Bristle flew up crying.
"Help! Help! Someone's stolen
my magic brush!"

"Sshh," Fingers calmed him.
"WHO'S stolen your magic brush?"
"The rats I expect!" cried Bristle.
"Reggie's always eyeing it!"
"Then I'll get it back for you,"
said Fingers. "You go on home,
before you spoil my plan!"

Chapter Five

At The Rats' House

Reggie Rat was in his garden,
rocking in a rocking chair,
when Fingers flew up.
"Fingers! This is a surprise!
What can we rats do for you?"

"A lot," said Fingers.

"We think you're taking things
from Miss Wand's shop.
That chair, for example.
And Bristle thinks you've taken
his magic brush!"

"Ah," said Reggie. "We'd love
a brush and pan like that.
But we don't have them. And this
chair? It was my grandfather's
before you fairies were even born!"

"Well, do you mind if I look inside?"
said Fingers.
Reggie was on his feet.
Rondo and Roxy blocked
the open door.
"We most certainly do!"
yelled Reggie.
"We don't poke around
in your house!
And you'll not meddle in ours!"

19

Fingers looked back down
the Forever Street path.
She could just see Pea and Pod
which meant Cyclone would be
close behind.

"All right," she said politely.
"Then I'll leave it to the
White Beast. He's right here.
And he'll be most interested to
find you have a chair made by
your grandfather exactly like
Miss Wand's!"

"The White Beast?" yelled Reggie.
"Coming here? Rondo, Roxy,
get your skates on!
We have an urgent meeting,
remember!"
And the rats were off,
leaving their front door wide open!

Chapter Six

What They Find

Cyclone stopped. He could sense
rats tearing through the grass.
But he was a lazy cat
and the fluttering fairies
were... oh... so close.
So he didn't chase the rats.

He kept on after Pea and Pod
right into the rats' garden.
"Quick!" called
Fingers. "In here!"
With a sigh of
relief the fairies
fluttered
to safety...

because, of course, Cyclone
couldn't get more than half a paw
through the rats' front door!

But he sniffed the rocking chair.
At once he recognised it
as the one from Miss Wand's
dolls' house.

And when the fairies managed
to push the dolls' piano out,
he recognised that too.

Feeling very pleased with himself,
he picked up the chair
and took it home to Miss Wand,
and then came back for the piano.
And, while he was busy,
Fingers, Pea and Pod hunted round
for Bristle's brush and pan.

First, Fingers held up her hands
and sang:
"Magic fingers if you can,
Feel out Bristle's brush and pan!"
Then she moved around the house,
knowing her fingers would tingle if
she got anywhere near them.

But they didn't.

Not once.

And it soon became clear,

the rats HADN'T stolen

Bristle's brush and pan…

or, if they had,

they weren't anywhere there!

Chapter Seven

In The Magic Cloud

"I don't know what we'll tell
Bristle," said Fingers, as she
and the twins hurried
back down Forever Street.
"He'll be so upset!"

"I'm not sure about that!" said Pea.

"Nor am I," said Pod, "Listen!"

Fingers stopped.

She could hear
Bristle laughing.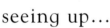

Next she saw him

playing on Elfie's

see-saw...

seeing up...

into the

magic cloud above.

"Fingers..." Elfie waved. "Bristle's playing. And having a good time!"

"I am!" laughed Bristle,
from up in the cloud.

"Right now I'm
seeing myself
as a sea-going fairy."
He sawed down
again, sending Elfie
seeing up.

31

"These clouds are amazing.
When you're up there, you see
yourself as something different.
You must have a go! It's magic!"

"I'd love to," said Fingers.
And soon, hearing Bristle's laughter,
all the other fairies came out
to join the fun... even Rainbow
in her nightdress.

And only when they'd all
had a turn seeing
into the magic clouds,
did they remember
the rats.

"Don't worry," said Fingers.
"Now they know the White Beast
is watching them. They won't
be stealing again in a hurry.
But I'm sorry, Bristle.
We didn't find your brush and pan."

"Oh dear!" Bristle's lip trembled.
"Now what'll I do...?"
He sat himself down hard
in a large clump of primroses
and immediately jumped up again.

"Ouch!" he yelled. "What was that?"
Elfie blushed.
Bristle was pulling out his brush
and pan!

"But who hid them there?"
cried Bristle.

Elfie hung his head.

"I did," he whispered. "I know
I shouldn't have but…"

"But WHY?" cried Fingers. "WHY?"

"Why do you think?" said Elfie.

"I know!" shouted Bristle.

"Because you knew if I didn't have
them I couldn't be busy
and I'd PLAY with you!"

"Exactly!" said Elfie.

"Will you forgive me?"

Bristle hugged Elfie.

"I will! I will!

Because I loved it.

But now... if you don't mind...

I must get busy!"

"Oh well," laughed Fingers,
"you can't separate fairies from
their magic for long, can you?"

"No," said Elfie. "You can't.
And I've another magic idea.
"Let's give those rats
a go on my see-saw.
It might do THEM some good too!"

So that's what they did
and the rats see-ed up
and saw themselves
as kind, honest and helpful.
And afterwards that's what
they tried to be... for a bit...
before they started
upsetting the hedgehogs!

"Oh dear," said Elfie.
"Now I suppose we'll have to
teach them another lesson!"
"Hmm," sighed Fingers.
"A fairy's work is never done!
Come on!"